A sea gull lands on the sand.

It stares at the bag
in my hand.

A Rookie reader®

Feeding the Gulls

Written by Deanna Calvert
Illustrated by George Ulrich

SCHOLASTIC INC.
New York Toronto London Auckland Sydney
Mexico City New Delhi Hong Kong Buenos Aires

To Carolyn and Kyle with love and gratitude, and also to Joan Broerman, whose selfless labor for Southern Breeze has launched the careers of so many children's writers. Joan is as essential to this book as sea gulls.

—D.C.

For Corry and Quinten

—G.U.

Reading Consultants

Linda Cornwell
Literacy Specialist

Katharine A. Kane
Education Consultant
(Retired, San Diego County Office of Education
and San Diego State University)

ISBN 0-516-24813-8

12 11 10 9 8 7 6 5 4 3 2 1 4 5 6 7 8 9/0

Printed in the U.S.A. 61

First Scholastic printing, May 2004

My bag is full of
soft white bread.

The sea gull
screeches to be fed.

I toss a slice of bread up high.

The sea gull snags it
from the sky.

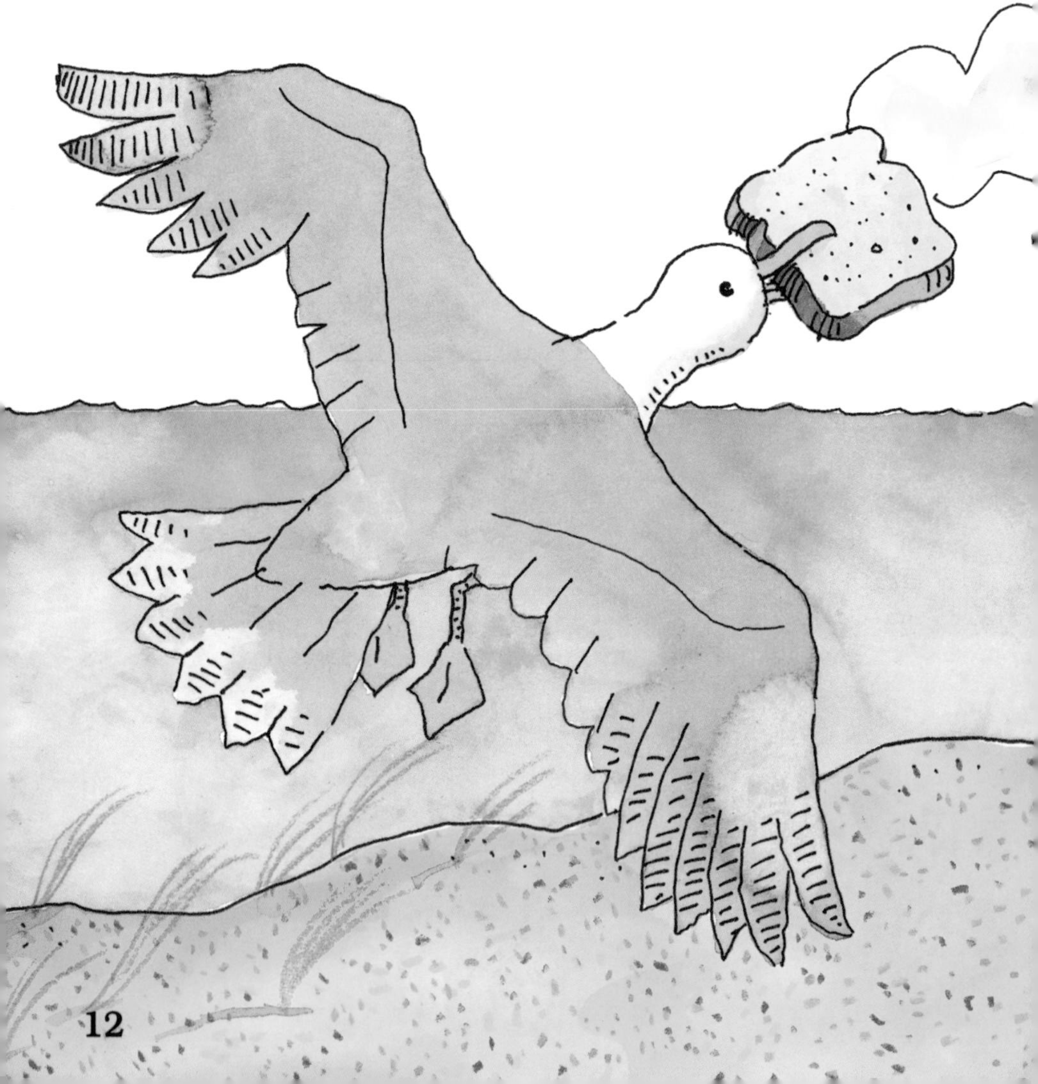

More gulls come.

Now there are twenty.

They call for bread.

I have plenty.

A white gull takes
bread from my hand.

I scatter slices on the sand.

More gulls come.

More and more.

I better go back to
the grocery store.

Word List (53 words)

a	fed	I	sand	takes
and	for	in	scatter	the
are	from	is	screeches	there
at	full	it	sea	they
back	go	lands	sky	to
bag	grocery	more	slice	toss
be	gull	my	slices	twenty
better	gulls	now	snags	up
bread	hand	of	soft	white
call	have	on	stares	
come	high	plenty	store	

About the Author

Deanna Calvert lives in Birmingham, Alabama, with her husband and daughter, dog, and cat. She used to teach college writing and literature courses, but now writes full time for children. Besides writing and spending time with her family, she enjoys fresh air and blue skies, trips to the zoo, and any kind of travel.

About the Illustrator

George Ulrich has been a children's book illustrator for 30 years. He lives in Marblehead, Massachusetts, with his wife, Suzanne.